LITTLE MISS DITZY

by Roger Hargreaves

TO:

_____

FROM:

_____

EAN

ISBN 978-0-8431-7690-2

9 780843 176902

5 04 99>

little Miss Ditzy

by Roger Hargreaves

PSS!
PRICE STERN SLOAN
An Imprint of Penguin Group (USA) Inc.

Welcome to Nonsenseland!

You may have heard of it!

It's where the trees are red and the grass is blue!

Where dogs wear hats and birds fly backwards!

And where Little Miss Ditzy lived, in the middle of Whoopee Wood.

Nonsenseland really is quite the most extraordinary place.

If you ever come across a worm wearing a straw boater and wearing a bow tie, you'll know you are in Nonsenseland!

And if you ever happen to catch sight of a pig playing tennis, you'll know exactly where you are!

Won't you?

That's right!

Nonsenseland.

One morning in January, little Miss Ditzy
was having breakfast,

A bowl full of marmalade, with milk and sugar!

While she ate, she was reading the
newspaper.

She read the *Nonsenseland Daily News*
every day, and always read it while she ate
her ditzy breakfast.

Something in the paper caught her eye!

She stopped eating and started reading.

The headline read:

"NONSENSE CUP WINNER"

And, underneath it said:

"This year's Nonsense Cup, for the silliest idea of the year (a green tree), was awarded yesterday to Mr. Silly by the King of Nonsenseland. Runners-up were Mr. Muddle and Mrs. Nincompoop."

"Next year," continued the story, "the Nonsense Cup will be awarded not for the silliest idea, but for the DOTTIEST idea of the year."

"The dottiest idea of the year?" little Miss Ditzy thought to her self as she popped a spoonful of marmalade into her mouth "I bet I could win that Nonsense Cup!"

After breakfast she set off for a walk in Whoopee Wood to think about this and that, but most of all to think about that famous Nonsense Cup.

On her walk, she met Mr. Silly.

"Congratulations on winning the Cup," she said to him.

"Oh it was nothing really," he replied modestly.

Little Miss Ditzy thought about telling him that she was going to enter next year, but then she decided not to.

January passed.

And February.

And Spring came, and the blue grass grew.

But, could little Miss Ditzy think of an idea?

She could not!
She just couldn't think of a single
dotty idea!

Summer came to Nonsenseland

And went!
Without a single dotty idea in mind!

And the red trees started to fall from the trees.

And then, one afternoon in late November,
little Miss Ditzy thought of her idea

The dottiest idea ever!

The year ended, and January arrived in Nonsenseland.

A huge crowd gathered as usual in the square to see who had won that year's Nonsense Cup.

The King of Nonsenseland mounted the specially built platform, and a hush descended on the crowd.

"Ladies and gentlemen," the King announced. "Again it is my pleasure to announce the annual winner of our famous Nonsense Cup."

"As you know," he continued, "the Cup will be awarded this year to whoever has had the dottiest idea of the year!"

The crowd held its breath.

"One of which," the King went on,
"has been entered by Mr. Nonsense!"

The crowd looked as Mr. Nonsense held up
his dotty idea for all to see,

A television set, with no screen!

"It's for people who don't like watching
television," he explained, proudly.

The crowd clapped.

"However," continued the King, "we have
an even dottier idea from last
year's winner!"

Mr. Silly triumphantly showed his invention to the crowd.

It was a clock!

"If you look at it in the mirror it tells you the right time," he announced.

The crowd cheered, and Mr. Silly felt sure that he was going to win the Nonsense Cup for the second year running.

"But," continued the King, and Mr. Silly realized that he wasn't.

"But," said the King again. "We did announce that the Nonsense Cup was to be awarded for the DOTTIEST idea of the year, and this year's winner has provided us with," he paused, "nine hundred and ninety nine DOTS!"

Little Miss Ditzy held her breath and blushed.

"Hurrah!" roared the crowd.

"Follow me," said the King.

The King and little Miss Ditzy led the crowd through Whoopee Wood to her cottage.

And there they stopped, and stared.

Little Miss Ditzy had spent the whole month of December painting dots all over her cottage. Hundreds and hundreds of different colored dots.

Nine hundred and ninety nine to be exact.

Little Miss Ditzy had counted them very carefully.

"That's a lot of dots," remarked the King as he handed over the Nonsense Cup, and the crowd cheered.

"Thank you, your Majesty," she replied, and blushed with pride.

Oh, one last thing!

If you are as good at counting dots as little
Miss Ditzy, you'll be interested to know
that there are one hundred and ninety three
small letter 'i's' in this story.

And there are one hundred and ninety three dots on
the top of all of them!

I should know!
Because I put them there!

ISBN 978-0-8431-7690-2

19 18 17 16 15 14 13 12 11 10

MR. MEN   LITTLE MISS

PSS!
PRICE STERN SLOAN

Little Miss Bossy

Little Miss Naughty

Little Miss Neat

Little Miss Sunshine

Little Miss Tiny

Little Miss Trouble

Little Miss Giggles

Little Miss Helpful

Little Miss Magic

Little Miss Shy

Little Miss Splendid

Little Miss Twins

Little Miss Chatterbox

Little Miss Ditzy

Little Miss Late

Little Miss Lucky

Little Miss Scatterbrain

Little Miss Star

Little Miss Busy

Little Miss Quick

Little Miss Wise

Little Miss Tidy

Little Miss Greedy

Little Miss Fickle

Little Miss Brainy

Little Miss Stubborn

Little Miss Curious

Little Miss Fun

Little Miss Contrary

Little Miss Somersault

$3.99 US
($4.99 CAN)

PSS!
PRICE STERN SLOAN

(Some titles may not
yet be available.)

ISBN 978-0-8431-7690-2

EAN

9 780843 176902